LUKA'S QUILT

GEORGIA GUBACK

GREENWILLOW BOOKS
NEW YORK

To R. B. W.,
and with special thanks to Maria and Bill,
Gaby, and Susan and Paul

PRINTED IN SINGAPORE BY TIEN WAH PRESS   FIRST EDITION   10 9 8 7 6 5 4 3 2

LIBRARY OF CONGRESS CATALOGING-IN-PUBLICATION DATA
GUBACK, GEORGIA.   LUKA'S QUILT / BY GEORGIA GUBACK.
P.   CM.
SUMMARY: WHEN LUKA'S GRANDMOTHER MAKES A TRADITIONAL HAWAIIAN QUILT FOR HER, SHE AND LUKA DISAGREE OVER
THE COLORS IT SHOULD INCLUDE.   ISBN 0-688-12154-3 (TRADE).   ISBN 0-688-12155-1 (LIB. BDG.)   [1. GRANDMOTHERS—
FICTION. 2. QUILTS—FICTION 3. HAWAII—FICTION.]   I. TITLE   PZ7.G9342LU 1994   [E]—DC20   93-12241 CIP AC

My tutu lives with us. Tutu. That's Hawaiian for grandmother. Tutu takes care of me while Mom and Dad work. We do lots of things together. I like that, and so does Tutu. But all that changed when the quilt came along.

One morning Tutu said, "I had a dream last night. I dreamed I was in a beautiful garden. There were flowers everywhere. It gave me an idea for a quilt. This quilt will be for you, Luka. I made a quilt for your mom. Now it's your turn."

"Will it have flowers on it?" I asked.

"Oh yes," Tutu replied. "It's a flower garden. There will be all kinds of flowers."

"It's going to be so pretty," I said.

"It will take a long time to make," said Tutu. "You'll have to be patient."

"That's okay," I said. "I can help."

After breakfast Tutu and I went to the fabric store.
"Choose a color," said Tutu.
There were so many pretty colors.
"I like that yellow," I said. "And that pink. And some of
that blue. And the lavender. And this orange is nice."
Tutu laughed. "Not so fast," she said. "Choose one
color. Just one."
"How can it be a flower garden if there's just one
color?" I asked.
"You'll see," said Tutu.
Just one color! Green. I chose green because flowers
have green leaves. The flower colors would come later.

Tutu sketched and cut and pinned and basted. And I got to help. This quilt is going to be so pretty, I kept thinking. I could hardly wait for the flowers.

At last Tutu put the quilt on the quilting frame. "Serious work now," she said. And I knew I wasn't big enough to help anymore.

"When are the flowers coming, Tutu?" I'd ask. She'd smile and answer, "You'll see, Luka. You'll see."

Then one day a long time after, Tutu took the quilt off the frame.
She ironed it and put it on my bed. "For you, Luka," she said.
The flowers! There were no flowers! "Where are the flowers?" I cried.
"Here," said Tutu. "See, here's amaryllis. And here's ginger.
And over there is jacaranda."
"Everything's white," I said. "How can there be flowers with no pretty
flower colors?"
"This is the way we make our quilts," said Tutu. "Two colors. It's our
Island tradition. You chose green, remember?"
"I thought the green was for leaves," I cried. "All the flowers in our
garden are in colors. It can't be a flower garden if the flowers are white."

Tutu's eyes got watery, and she quietly turned and went to her room and shut the door.
I looked at Tutu's quilt again. I thought it was going to be so pretty, and all it was was white.

I sat down and cried.

Things changed after that. Tutu and I used to be such good friends. Now we had nothing to say to each other. We didn't do things together anymore. And all because of that quilt. It's going to stay like this forever, I thought. It was awful.

But Tutu surprised me. A few days later she said, "Today is Lei Day. You've never been to a Lei Day celebration, Luka. Let's declare a truce and see what's going on at the park."

"What's a truce?" I asked.

"That's when people put aside their differences and come together again for a little while," Tutu answered.

I didn't see how that was going to work, but it was worth a try. "Okay," I said.

I filled the water jug, and Tutu got the tatami mat, and we stopped at Aiko's to buy bento for our picnic. By the time the bus came, it was almost beginning to feel like old times.

There was so much going on at the park. We listened to the music. We watched the dancing. We spread our mat under a tree and ate our bento. And Tutu treated me to shave ice.

Later we came to a place where kids were making leis.
"Come," said a lady. "Make a lei."
"Is it okay, Tutu?" I asked.
"Go ahead," said Tutu.
    The lady got me started. She gave me a long needle and strong thread and showed me how to string the flowers together.

There were all kinds of blossoms. They were in cardboard boxes with wet newspapers all around to keep them fresh. I chose a pink flower. Next I added a yellow. Then an orange. And then a lavender. Tutu laughed. "No, not that way, Luka," she said. "Choose one color, maybe two. But no more than two."

I could feel myself getting angry, and I tried not to. I was remembering our truce.

"Tutu," I said, "it's my lei."

"But…," Tutu began. Then she stopped. She was remembering our truce, too, and she didn't say another word.

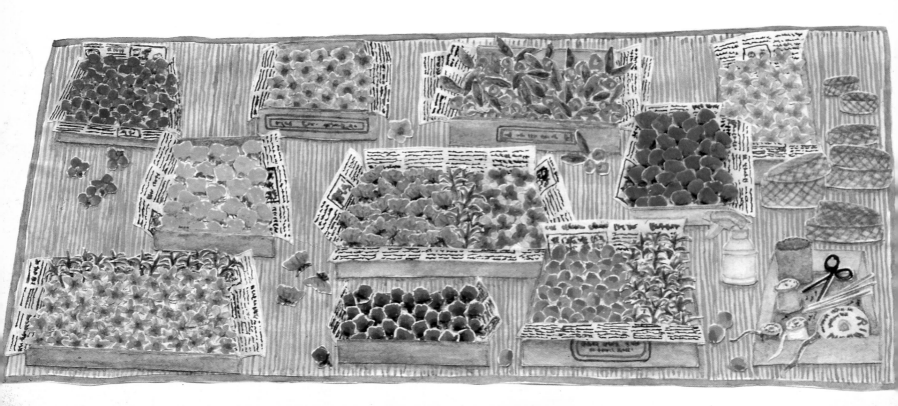

Things got better at once. I didn't feel angry anymore, and I made my lei my way. It turned out very pretty, and I got to keep it and wear it home.

So the truce worked, and I felt happy. "I'm glad you had that truce idea, Tutu," I said. "I had a good time."

"So did I," Tutu answered.

By bedtime the happy feeling was still with me. I looked at Tutu's quilt again. Maybe a white flower garden wasn't so bad. I snuggled underneath her quilt and fell asleep.

The next day Tutu said, "Luka, I was looking at your lei last night. I saw your flower garden in it, and it gave me an idea."

I got to help with Tutu's idea. I chose pretty flower colors from her scrap baskets, and then I helped sketch and cut and baste. Then Tutu did the sewing and quilting.

A long time later, after my pretty flower lei had dried out and turned brown, Tutu called me. We went to my bedroom. And there they were—like magic! All the flowers I had dreamed of in a special quilted lei!

"Just for you, Luka," said Tutu. "Now you have all your flowers and all your colors."

"Oh, it's so pretty!" I cried.

And all at once I was hugging Tutu and she was hugging me back. And everything was better again.

I like my quilt a lot now. Sometimes I have it plain—my white flower garden. And sometimes I put Tutu's quilted lei on top and have my flower garden in color. I like it both ways. But what I like most is that Tutu and I are friends again. And I can tell Tutu likes that best of all, too.